Sal thing

Habi Akinteye
Illustrated by Rista Khatun

TUEMS Children's Books

For Phoebe, Hadassah, Elkanah, Erina & Inara - HA

First published in Great Britain by TUEMS Children's Books in 2020

ISBN: 978-1-916-05745-6

Text and illustration copyright © Habi Akinteye 2020

TUEMS Children's Books is an imprint of TUEMS Publishing

A CIP catalogue record for this book is available from the British Library.

Visit our website at:
www.tuemspublishing.co.uk

Icons of lined hut, hen, confused face, water well, hand with cuffs taken from Flaticon.com by Smachicons, Freepik Surang, and Itim2010
Hut icon on chapter one from Clipart Library
Other icons from Microsoft Clipart
Translation on Google Translate and Duolingo
Translation checked and confirmed by Emily Jean

Contents

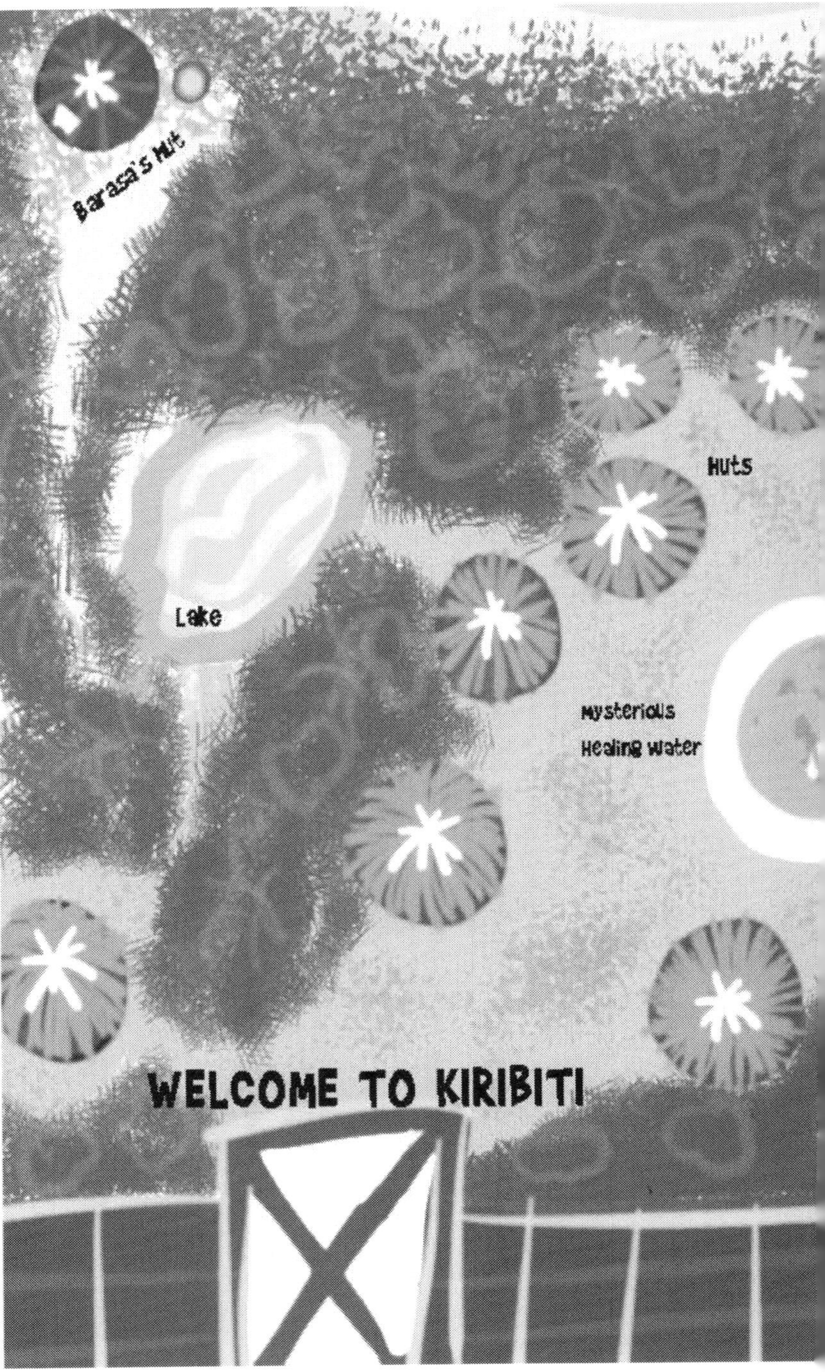
Barasa's Hut
Huts
Lake
Mysterious
Healing Water
WELCOME TO KIRIBITI

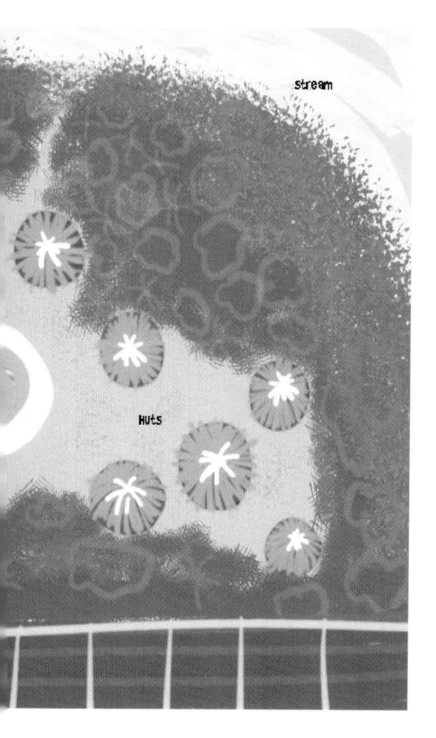

CHAPTER 1

KIRIBITI

A small village

Kiribiti is a tranquil, beautiful, and a friendly little village, where everyone smiles, laughs, dances and eats together. Neighbouring villages long to have such a peaceful community as Kiribiti.

Some admire their unity, others envy their sincere love for one another. A large number of people try their hardest to move into this seemingly earthly **PARADISE,** but Kiribiti would not just open its gate for anybody to come in. They are careful about people who may not mean well for others.

Crops grow and are ripe for harvest before the fullness of their time.

Mysterious healing water flows from the rock in the centre of the village.

Fowls, cattle, pigs, and sheep are reared together, and they multiply quickly.

KIRIBITI IS LIKE A LITTLE HEAVEN.

Almost everyone in Kiribiti is either a farmer or a hunter. They are hardworking people and early risers. Before the cockerels crow at dawn, they are up and running. There is nobody among them that is lazy. But as busy as they get, they still create time for their families.

At night, the entire village gathers together to eat supper. They gather in groups and each group eats from one pot. After the meal, the elders share moonlight tales with the children.

One evening after meal, Mzee Alamini brings the children together and tells them a story.

"Once upon a time...," says Mzee Alamini " *...Many, many years ago, there was a man who came into Kiribiti at night.*

He was bruised and battered. He walked with rickety legs that were dripping blood. It was obvious that he was almost dying, and after a little while, he fell to the ground. A woman saw him where he laid on the ground at the entrance of the village. He was about to take his last breath. The woman shouted out for help and many people gathered and took the man to a herbal clinic. They bound his wounds and gave him herbs to drink. The women cooked good food for him, the men looked after his wounds. Three days later, the man began to heal. He said to the villagers who were present with him, 'You didn't know who I am or what I am, and you all received me and showed me this

great *kindness. In return, I will...'*
Mzee Alamini pauses.

"I will...what? Don't pause like that, Mzee Alamini," Shouts a bold voice of a girl from the audience. "**GRRR...** I don't like suspense."

"Salama! **BOLD** as a tiger! Where is your patience? Suspense makes stories more exciting and fun. It gives you something to think about."

"Oh Mzee, I know, I know... but please what happens next... it's almost bedtime. They will call us to bed in a minute." Salama replies.

"Yes, you are right, the moon is moving away. It will be dark soon," Mzee Alamini continues...

"*Back to the story... The man said, 'I will reward Kiribiti bountifully that this generation and the generations to come will enjoy.' The man looked up to the sky, closed his eyes and...*"

"**Salama!!!** It's time for bed!" Shouts a voice from a distance.

"**OH NO! IT'S MAMA FIFI. NOW, I AM GOING TO MISS THE REST OF THE STORY.**" Says Salama.

"**Feye... Akeyo... Gathii**" different voices shout for other children to come to bed.

All the children got up and ran to their huts.

"Hope you will finish the story tomorrow, Mzee Alamini, I cannot wait! Good night Baba," says Salama as she dashes off to her grandma's hut.

I wonder what the man did when he looked up to the sky and closed his eyes. See, this is the reason why I hate suspense.

It will be on my mind all night.

Salama has this thought running through her mind.

CHAPTER 2

STRANGE HAPPENINGS

why these?

The following day, just before nightfall, children are out playing. Some adults have just returned from the farm relaxing outside. Some are playing Mancala game with each other. Laughter, joy, and happiness were bouncing everywhere in the air.

Suddenly, a strange scream and wail interrupt the joyful noise. This has never happened before. Everyone playing stops in shock and trembles, with their eyes wide open and their ears pricked up.

"What's that noise?" They ask each other.

"HELP US!"

A loud voice of a man panicking booms.

"THERE IS A STRANGE THING IN THE VILLAGE! HELP!"

A woman shouts as she outruns the man who initially cried for help. The panic grows as another woman carrying a basket on her head and a baby on her back almost falls as she tries to escape from whatever it was, she saw.

The men playing Mancala shiver in terror, they jump up, fling the Mancala in the air and run for their lives.

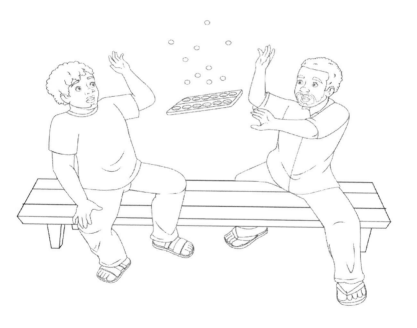

The young girls coming from the stream with a pot of water balanced on their heads, suddenly chuck the pots away!

Everywhere is in complete disarray.

"IT'S A BIG FOX! RUN FOR YOUR LIVES!" Cries a young boy as he runs home.

"IT'S A MONSTER!"

A man shouts as he sprints past.

"WHAT? WHAT?!" Salama panics. "Mama Fifi, get up, get in! There is something in the village."

Mama Fifi is a deep sleeper. She doesn't hear a single scream or shout. She is fast asleep outside on a woven mat, after eating a bowl of Ugali with sauce and beef, enjoying the cool breeze from the stream nearby.

Mama Fifi runs inside confused. "What's going on? What's going on?" she stutters.

Brave Salama runs towards where everyone is running from. She needs to check on her friends, Siti and Jelani. She wants to be sure they are safe.

Siti is already in bed sleeping.

Jelani is on the watch outside. He has his helmet on his head and a big stick in his hand. He is ready to whack whatever shows up in front of his hut.

Jelani hears a rattling sound coming from the bush. He switches on his helmet's light and moves towards it, aiming the stick in a way ready to hit.

The movement is getting closer, Jelani is sweating.

"HE-HAA!" He swings the stick.

"HEY! WAIT! WAIT!! NI MIMI SALAMA, NI MIMI!" Salama yells out.

"OH, SALAMA! IT'S YOU! YOU CREPT UP ON ME!" Shouts Jelani. "What are you looking for this dangerous night? I was close to whacking your head."

"Crept up? I didn't creep up on you. I was running to come and tell you that there is a strange thing in the village. No-one knows what it is." Says Salama.

"What did they say it looks like? I heard it looks like a big dog." Says Jelani.

"I'm hearing different things, Jelani. Some people are saying it looks like a fox. Others said it looked like a monster! Now I don't know," replies Salama.

"WE NEED TO FIND OUT WHAT IT IS AND STOP IT!"

"STOP IT? ARE YOU BEING SERIOUS?" Jelani shouts.

"Tomorrow morning, we go out into the bush and look everywhere for it or look for a clue of what it is. Siti is good at solving puzzles, she will be a great help. **GO INSIDE JELANI, STAY SAFE!"** Says Salama as she rushes back home.

"Moo-hoo-hoo-haa-haa..."

A voice echoes from the forest.

"Run Salama, run!"

shouts Jelani as he quickly runs inside his hut.

Salama runs as fast as she could. She trips on a log of wood on the ground. It's too dark to see. She picks herself up and continues to run.

The sound of owls hooting and foxes howling creates more panic in little Salama's heart. Home seems to be getting farther and farther away. Finally, she gets to her hut, panting like a deer.

Salama's eyes remain wide open in terror as she curls up beside Mama Fifi.

She is just drifting off to sleep slowly when she hears a sound...

"ZZZZZ, CHRRRCHRRR, ZZZZ..."

Salama jumps up and says,

"OH NO! I NEARLY DIED."

She doesn't know whether to smile or cry. Her heart almost leapt out of her mouth. It's Mama Fifi snoring. Mama Fifi's snores are as loud as a cathedral bell of years back.

Salama lifts Mama Fifi's jaw to close her mouth to stop her from snoring. As she pushes it up it drops back down, up, down, up, down. **SALAMA GIVES UP!**

She reaches for her scarf, wraps it around her head to cover both ears. "Thank goodness! The snoring is fading away," She heaves a big sigh of relief. Salama then falls asleep.

Salama's sleep is interrupted at midnight by a wailing sound from afar. Salama jumps up in fear.

"Did I just hear something? What is that again?" Salama speaks as she moves closer to the window. She is too scared to peep. She crawls and moves her ear close to the muddy wall.

"MOTO! MOTO! MSAADA!!!"

Someone shouts in Swahili.

Followed by a strange continuous echoing,

'PAA-PAA-TA-TA-TA'

"FIRE!" Salama exclaims.
"WHERE? THIS MUST BE A WILDFIRE." She wonders.

"Mama Fifi, get up! There is a fire. Someone is shouting 'fire'!"

Mama Fifi is still half-asleep and half-awake but when she heard some heavy footsteps of people running helter-skelter shouting 'Msaada! (Fire!)', her eyes open wide and bright. She shakes in fear, asking "where, where?'" She is confused.

Salama and Mama Fifi run out of their hut.

All the farmlands are on fire!

"HELP US STOP IT BEFORE IT GETS TO THE HUTS!" shouts a terrified woman with two babies in her hands and three young children clinging to her legs.

"Who is responsible for this?" Asks Mama Fifi.

"Hmm, I think I know," Salama replies tapping her index finger against her lips as she thinks.

All the men in the village come together and decide what to do to stop the fire. They quickly light their fire torches and run to the stream to fetch water to stop the fire.

The women and the children gather in one place and wonder what is going on in Kiribiti.

Last night, there was a strange thing in the village, now fire.

Fear grips the heart of everyone. They switch their head from right to left at every little sound.

The men try their hardest to put out the fire. They eventually extinguish it.

The cockerel crows,

'COCK-A-DOODLE-DOO'.

It is morning. No-one had a wink of sleep. Everyone in the village gathers together. One eagerly looking at the other's face, expecting an explanation about the occurrence. But no-one knows what started the fire that burned down all the crops.

All the maize burned and turned to popcorns. That explains the *paa-paa-ta-ta-ta'* sound. All the corns were popping. Everywhere looks like it has rained popcorn. The tea farm, coffee, rice, millet, potatoes, cassava, wheat, bananas, and beans burned down.

"WE ARE GOING TO STARVE TO DEATH. THERE IS NOTHING LEFT TO EAT."

Mumbi, the wife of the village chief cries out. She bursts into tears.

All the villagers look sad, many put their hands on their head, some just hang their heads in sorrow.

Then, Mzee Alamini breaks the silence. "What happened last night? What entered our village that brought along this misfortune? We cannot just fold our arms and do nothing. We need to get to the root of this." He says convincingly. The villagers nod in agreement.

"Can everyone bring all the food they have in their huts and barns together in one place? We eat all meals together from now on. It's a tough time for all of us, we have to ration well until we can get help from the neighbouring villages. There will be no extra meals for some months." Okello, the village chief commands. The villagers agree.

While the meeting is still going on, Salama, Siti, and Jelani tiptoe out of the gathering.

They plan to go and look for the uninvited guest who probably brought this havoc.

The three friends search everywhere for clues. They come back at midday to check if there has been any information. Everyone still seems to be in a state of confusion.

Siti suggests they go and look some more; they may have missed something.

CHAPTER 3

WEIRD CREATURE

A puzzle to solve

It's now getting dark.

"We should go home now," says Salama. "It will not be good for us to stay out here in the forest till it's dark, we may not find our way home. And who knows what they saw last night and whatever that was that burned down all the farms?"

"Why don't we go different directions and see if we find anything or any trail on the way?" Jelani suggests.

"THAT IS SUCH A BAD IDEA, JELANI! WE SHOULD STICK TOGETHER." Says Salama.

"I have always thought you are the brave one, Salama. **YOU ARE THE GIRL OF THE FOREST.** You know everywhere in this jungle. You have single-handedly knocked out a fox once, Salama. I don't believe you are afraid now." Siti says as she smiles.

"Ok then, you take a stick. Have your fire torch lit, hold it with your other hand. Anything shows up, whack it and run." Salama orders.

The friends part ways.

TWOOWUT, CHIRP CHIRP, WOOHOO WOOHOO.

The sound of the forest animals and birds intensifies.

CRACK...   CRACK...
CREEK...   CREEK   sound

comes from the bush behind Salama as if someone is creeping behind her. Salama switches around swiftly.

"WHO IS THAT? WHAT'S THAT?" Salama asks anxiously.

"Onyesha uso wako! You'd better show your face!"

Salama waves the fire torch and the big stick at the same time as if she wants to do karate fight.

MOO-HA-HA-HA

echoes around Salama.

Something moves fast in front of her.

"HEY! STOP! WHAT ARE YOU? DON'T PLAY TRICKS ON ME. I AM SO NOT INTERESTED." Salama stands still, looking angry and feisty.

"WAJ IT YOU WHO BURNED DOWN OUR FARMJ, UH?"

Salama asks.

KEKEKEKE-MOOHAHAHA

A voice echoes.

A swift movement again in front of Salama.

"I can see you. You have a **LONG BEAK.** Are you a bird?"

Fearless Salama asks curiously.

"Mo-koo-kaka..."

It moves fast again behind Salama. She turns around quickly. She catches another glimpse.

"**HAA-HA**, I saw you. You have two **HORNS**. Are you a buffalo?" Says Salama.

Vooo - Swift movement again.

"You're still here? Oh! I see… **HUMPS, HUMPS**… Are you a camel?" Now Salama is confused. She cannot comprehend what she just saw. She begins to panic. She

wants to run but she doesn't know
where the weird creature is hiding.

HAHAHAHA
NENDA-A-A-A

The voice booms.

"Nenda? You mean 'go'? Are you
telling me to go? You speak Swahili?

NOW SHOW YOUR FACE!
I AM NOT SCARED OF
YOU ANYMORE!" Shouts

Salama.

"HAPANA-A-A-A..."

the voice echoes and vanishes into

the distance.

"NO? YOU COWARD! BE GONE FOREVER!"

Salama exclaims.

She runs home.

"I hope Jelani and Siti are okay."
She speaks to herself.

"Mama Fifi, Mama Fifi, where are you, Mama? I saw a thing," Salama shouts as she runs towards her hut.

"Where have you been, Salama? I have been worried sick about you. Siti's mum and Jelani's mum have been here looking for Siti and Jelani. I have been so worried that my tummy has been unsettled. And so are your friends' mums. We have been having many scary thoughts; maybe you've been eaten by the strange creature in the village, maybe you have been stolen, many bad thoughts were running through our minds." Mama Fifi says, looking all disturbed.

"Erm, Mama Fifi, I am sorry. We went into the forest," says Salama as she hangs her head in shame.

"MSITU? FOREST, SALAMA? KWANINI, WHY? Mama Fifi asks. She looks terrified.

"I am sorry, Mama Fifi, we went to see if we could find a trail of the thing that scared the villagers off last night. It is very likely that it was responsible for the fire." Salama explains.

"OH NO! YOU ARE TOO LITTLE FOR THAT, SALAMA. YOU ARE

ONLY TEN YEARS OLD. WHERE ARE YOUR FRIENDS, NOW?" Asks Mama Fifi.

"They should be home by now, I hope." Salama cringes.

"**REALLY?** You're not sure where they are? Let's go to their huts right away!" Mama Fifi and Salama hurry out.

They get to Siti's hut. She is already in trouble and not allowed to go out to play for two days.

Jelani has just been grounded too. He is not allowed to go out to play for some days.

"**NOW YOU ARE GROUNDED AS WELL.**" says Mama Fifi to Salama.

Salama goes to bed feeling sad. She feels defeated and thinks the strange creature will strike again and do more harm in the village.

CHAPTER 4

OH! WHERE ARE THE CHILDREN?

More strange happenings

In the morning, Salama goes to fetch some drinking water. She helps Mama Fifi with the chores and follows her to the farm to help with raking, soiling and ridging the fields, getting them ready for new planting.

As they plough the ground, Mama Fifi asks, "What was it you were saying you saw in the forest last night?"

Salama's eyes light up. She couldn't believe Mama Fifi or anyone would want to know now that they are all under punishment.

"Yes, Mama Fifi. Let me get a chalk and a slate, I need to draw it." Salama responds. "See, Mama Fifi, it's a weird-looking creature. Very weird, grandma. I have never seen anything like it before. It has a beak like a bird. It has two horns like a buffalo, two humps like a camel, fur all over it like a gorilla, and ears like a rabbit. It even said a word of Swahili - Nenda, he said 'nenda' Mama Fifi,"

"Hmmm, this is rather strange," Says Mama Fifi. "Very strange, I pray for Kiribiti. It shall be safe again. That thing shall be exposed."

"Amina, Mama Fifi, amen." Says Salama.

"**HELP US! HELP!** Two children are missing. They went to the stream to fetch water with other kids. They were all walking together and all of a sudden two of them got snatched from behind." Cries out a woman looking distressed and terrified.

"THREE MORE KIDS HAVE BEEN REPORTED MISSING AT THE OTHER SIDE OF THE STREAM. WE DON'T KNOW WHAT IS SNATCHING THE

CHILDREN!" Exclaims a man running past.

"I need to see Siti and Jelani. I need to beg Mama Siti and Mama Jelani, I need to talk to my friends. We need to put a stop to this chaos." Salama says to herself.

"I'LL BE BACK SOON, MAMA FIFI," says Salama as she dashes off.

Before Mama Fifi could ask where Salama was going, she'd already gone.

"This girl will not give me a heart attack, I pray. I hope she doesn't go near the forest or the stream." Says Mama Fifi, looking fed up.

"Jelani, Siti! Where are you? **NJO INJE! COME OUT! CHILDREN ARE GOING MISSING!"** Shouts Salama as she storms into Siti's hut.

Siti jumps up from where she was sitting making colourful beaded necklaces.

"ARE YOU SERIOUS?"

Replies Siti.

"NO WAY!" Says Jelani

as he quickly drops the clothes he was about to hang on the washing line. Siti and Jelani are neighbours. It is always easy to hear what they are saying in Siti's hut from Jelani's backyard.

"Where is Mama Siti and Mama Jelani? We need to apologise for the other day because now, we all need to come up with a plan. " Says Salama.

"They're in the back-garden planting crops." Siti replies.

"Mama Siti, Mama Jelani, we are so sorry for what we did the other day. Please forgive us, I need my friends back." Salama pleads.

"Hahaha, Salama, you need your friends back? Salama, bwana bibi, boss lady. You are forgiven, but be careful, all of you. Says Mama Siti. Mama Jelani nods in agreement.

"Thank you Mama Siti, thank you Mama Jelani, we love you!" The three friends say together at once, as they run to Salama's hut.

The friends sit down together and talk about what Salama saw the other night.

"I wonder what that thing was. It has **FUR** all over, **TWO HORNS LIKE A BUFFALO, HUMPS LIKE A CAMEL**, a **BEAK LIKE A BIRD** and **EARS LIKE A RABBIT**. Could it be the same thing snatching the children? Salama asks curiously.

"Hmm, this is a puzzle for us to solve. **I THINK IT IS A MONSTER.** What do you think, Jelani?" Asks Siti.

"It must be! Where has this monster come from? Our village has never known anything like this. Kiribiti has always been peaceful. How can we make all these to stop?" Curious Jelani asks.

"That's why I brought us here, Jelani. We need to stop whatever it is. We need to bring peace back to Kiribiti. Whatever it takes," says Salama, bravely.

"How do you intend to do that, Salama? How?" Asks Siti.

"I will go to the other side of the stream. That is where some children were snatched. I will carefully go and see if I can see any footprints or trails." Salama explains her plans.

"YOU'RE NOT BEING SERIOUS, SALAMA. YOU MUST BE KIDDING US. WE HAVE JUST COME OFF BEING GROUNDED, NOW YOU WANT TO GET US INTO BIGGER TROUBLE. YOU WANT TO GO SOMEWHERE AGAIN? SOMEWHERE WHERE CHILDREN ARE BEING SNATCHED BY GOD-KNOWS-WHAT? COUNT ME OUT OF YOUR PLANS, SALAMA,

I AM *SORRY.*" Siti responds angrily.

"Are you with me, Jelani?" Salama turns to Jelani.

"I guess you are on your own on this, Salama. I don't want to get into trouble." Replies Jelani.

"BOTH OF YOU ARE BACKING OUT ON ME, RIGHT? KWELI? REALLY? AJANTE, THANK YOU!" Says Salama sarcastically. She leaves their presence in annoyance and goes for a walk.

Salama sulks as she walks along a pathway in the bush. She puts her hands on her back and hangs her head. She walks slowly and dejected.

SMACK! SPLAT!

Something lands on Salama's head.

"OUCH! WHAT IS... THAT?"

Salama cries out. She looks up to see where that came from.

"IT'S YOU! SILLY MONKEY!" She shouts.

A monkey hanging on a tree threw two banana peels on Salama's head.

The monkey chuckles. He is having

so much fun. He peels another

banana, swallows it in a flash, and tries to chuck the peel at Salama again.

"NENDA, SILLY TUMBILI!" Salama yells

at him. The monkey did not move. Instead, he put his hands over his mouth and giggles away. Salama picks up a little stone from the ground to throw at the monkey, just to scare him off. When Salama picks the stone up, the monkey hides, when she put it down, the monkey pops out. The monkey wants to play hide and seek.

Salama realises the monkey wants to play. **"NOT TODAY TUMBILI, NOT TODAY,"** Salama says to the monkey as she walks up the hill.

SCREEECHHH...

A deafening noise of the monkey screeching. The cry disappears into thin air.

"WHAT'S THAT?
TUMBILI?
MONKEY?

HEY, HEY!"

Salama runs after the fading cry.

"STOP!   WAIT!"

Salama runs, even though she cannot see anything.

The monkey is far gone.

"IF YOU HURT THAT POOR TUMBILI,

I AM NEVER GOING TO FORGIVE YOU, WHATEVER YOU ARE!"

Salama shouts as she runs.

CHAPTER 5

A CREEPY OLD HUT

So So Creepy

Salama is tired. She sits on a big stone and weeps like a baby.

"IT'S MY FAULT! I SHOULD HAVE PLAYED

WITH THE MONKEY. I SHOULD HAVE TAKEN HIM WITH ME. NOW, HE IS SNATCHED AWAY.

Maybe the monster has eaten him.

BOOHOOHOOHOO."

She sobs.

A faint sound of wailing drifts in with the wind. Some voices cry out.

"Heeelp! Get us out, please... Can anybody hear us?"

Salama has walked far away from home. She is now on the other side of the stream without noticing. She listens and follows the voices.

She walks deeper and deeper into the woods.

Salama looks up and sees an abandoned hut. She runs up the hill to see if that is where the noise was coming from. The hut looks dilapidated and creepy.

Salama gets to the hut. Everywhere looks dirty and stinks badly like cows' dung.

She becomes so curious, she enters inside, clipping her nose together with her two fingers.

There are skulls of animals hung on the wall and skins of deer. Everything in the hut looks creepy. Salama's eyes catch something that looks very familiar. She freezes for a second, her eyes pop out.

"WHAT? THIS LOOKS LIKE WHAT I SAW IN THE BUSH THE OTHER DAY."

Salama moves closer to the hanging on the wall, to see it properly.

"YES, IT IS... FUR..."

She strokes it.

"YES, HUMPS... A BEAK... OH, IT'S A COSTUME! WAIT A MINUTE, A COSTUME! SOMEONE IS WEARING IT."

Salama speaks out. She quickly covers her mouth with her hands. *Someone may be around* - she thinks to herself.

She dashes out of the hut and sprints
back to the village.

"**SITI, JELANI, COME OUT! THERE IS SOMETHING I NEED TO TELL YOU. I SAW A STRANGE THING TODAY!**" Salama exclaims.

The two friends run out. They are happy to see Salama. They thought she was no longer their friend.

"What did you see again this time, Salama?" Jelani asks excitedly.

"First, I was going, then came a bang on my head, then I looked up. It was a silly tumbili..." Salama narrates.

"A MONKEY?" Siti is interested, she wants to know more.

Salama continues, "...Then I shooed the monkey away, but he wanted to play hide and seek. I was not in the mood, so I ignored him and walked off. "

Suddenly, the monkey screeched so loud and his cry faded into the distance.

You won't believe this, something snatched him!"

"REALLY?" Asks Jelani.

"I followed the cry into the forest, then I got tired. I sat down blaming myself for what had happened to the monkey. Out of the blue, I heard a faint noise of people crying out for help. They sounded like children. So, I got up and followed the noise up the hill. I looked up and I saw a creepy old hut standing alone at the very top of the horizon. I ran up the hill and entered the hut. I saw many creepy things, but the most amazing of all, was one strange thing. It was exactly like that thing I saw in the forest the other day. The only difference now is that it was hung on the wall, it was a costume." Salama explains.

"OOH," says Siti. **"I KNOW! THE STRANGE THING IN THE VILLAGE IS A PERSON. I MEAN SOMEONE IS WEARING A COSTUME AS A DISGUISE. HE MUST HAVE BURNED THE FARMS TOO. HE PROBABLY KIDNAPPED THE CHILDREN AND STOLE THE MONKEY."**

"Sawasawa, Siti. **EXACTLY!"** Replies Salama.

"What are your plans now, Salama? Asks Jelani.

"I am going back, friends." Says Salama.

"ARE YOU OUT OF YOUR MIND? YOU CANNOT GO BACK THERE, IT'S NOT SAFE." Says Siti.

"If I don't go back there, who will save those people crying? I cannot tell an adult because they will not believe me. I will probably get into bigger trouble if I tell them I have been into the forest. I'd go and save those people. Whatever happens, I'd bear the consequence. Pray for me!" Salama picks up her backpack and a long stick. She runs out of the hut.

"Wait, Salama, wait!" Siti and Jelani run after her. "We will wait for you at the edge of the forest." Says the two friends.

"That's fine! See you soon, Siti. See you soon, Jelani."

CHAPTER 6

THE WONKY MAN

Wonder who He is

It is already 3.15 pm.

Salama runs into the forest. She can still hear the wailing sound of people crying for help. She hides behind the creepy hut and peeps out. She checks if anyone is around. After a short time, she hears footsteps coming towards the hut. Salama freezes. Her eyes move like a pendulum from side to side.

"Oh my, oh my." She whispers.

Salama creeps further out to see what was approaching.

THE FOOTSTEPS ARE HEAVIER AND LOUDER.

IT'S COMING CLOSE.

"Oh! It's someone." She slinks back into hiding.

It is a wonky-looking man with a hunch back. He has a very long nose that looks plastered to his thin face and long legs that look like they are attached to his bony body.

He walks up to something that looks like a well, opens it and throws a flatbread in it.

It is a well but there is no water inside it.

"SHUT UP!"

He shouts at the people crying in the well.

"TOMORROW I WILL EAT YOU ALL. I NEED SOME FLESH ON MY BONES, HEHEHEHE."

He laughs devilishly and closes the well.

He walks towards the hut.

Now Salama panics more. She wishes the ground could open for her to hide in it. She closes her eyes and says some words of prayer. Then, she hears a door shut. **"PHEW,"** She heaves a big sigh. **"THAT WAS CLOSE."** She says.

Now, the wonky man is snoring.

Salama thinks to herself...

If I go back to the village and tell Mama Fifi or the villagers what I saw, they will not believe me, but if

I go back with these people in the well, they will believe me. Let me try to rescue them.

As Salama raises her right leg to tiptoe, something jumps on her.

IT'S THE MONKEY!

"TUMBILI, IT'S YOU," She whispers. "It's so good to see you again. I thought something bad has happened to you."

"EEEK-AAK-EEK!" Squeaks the monkey. He sits on Salama's left shoulder.

"SHUSH, QUIET TUMBILI.

If the wonky man hears us, we're

DOOMED." Salama smiles as she

strokes the monkey.

She tiptoes to the well, opens it and

whispers, **"UNAWEZA KUNISIKIA?**
CAN YOU HEAR ME? HELLO,
HELLO."

"Hey, kuna mtu hapa. Someone is

here. Wake up!" Says a voice from

the well.

"My name is Salama. I have come

to help you. We are quietly going

to get out of here. I repeat, quietly.

The wonky man is sleeping." Salama explains.

Salama dips her hand into her backpack and brings out a long rope. She ties the rope to a tree stump and throws the other end of the rope into the well. They climb out one after the other.

There are twelve children in total. They quietly walk out of the forest, and Salama and the monkey lead them back into the village.

Siti and Jelani are surprised to see Salama with the twelve children.

"KAZI NZURI SALAMA, GOOD JOB!"

Siti and Jelani shout in great delight.

The children clap and sing:

 Salama is our hero.

They sing it over and over again, dancing around her.

All the villagers start coming out one by one.

"WHAT'S HAPPENING?"

They wonder.

They all follow Salama to the chief's hut as she takes the lead.

Many mums and dads are happy to see their children back. They cannot wait to give them big hugs and cuddles.

CHAPTER 7

THE ARREST

The Reason Must Be Known

Okello, the chief, asks Salama what happened and where she got the children from.

Salama explains everything to the chief and everyone listens. They all stare with their mouths agape.

"WHO IS THIS WONKY MAN? GUARDS, MEN, I WANT YOU TO FOLLOW SALAMA INTO THE FOREST AND GET ME THAT MAN RIGHT AWAY. BRING THAT COSTUME ALONG AS WELL." Okello orders.

All the men and the guards march into the forest. They find the man making fire. He is getting ready to cook the children. He doesn't know that they have already escaped.

"YOU'RE UNDER ARREST!"

A guard shouts out.

"WHAT HAVE I DONE?"

The wonky man demands.

He tries to run away but he wobbles. The men quickly catch up with him and carry him to the village as he throws a big tantrum.

Everyone looks at him and asks one another,

"EYYY, IS THAT NOT BARASA, THE EXILED ONE? WHY HAS HE DONE THIS? "

Okello is surprised to see that the wonky man is Barasa.

Okello asks him,

"WHY DID YOU BURN THE FARMS? WHY DID YOU STEAL OUR CHILDREN? WHY WERE YOU CREATING PANICS IN OUR VILLAGE? WHY THIS COSTUME,

Baraſa? I demand an anſwer."

Barasa hangs his head in shame, and says, "You people banished me from my ancestors' sweat. My ancestor came into this village many years ago, though he was dying when he came and you people of Kiribiti accepted him, and saved his life. He blessed you in return. He gave you plenty of money and livestock and a crystal which he asked you to put in your waters so that it can heal you from diseases when you drink from it. My ancestors brought all their goodies and fortunes into Kiribiti. They made Kiribiti a happy, healthy, rich and fruitful place. They made Kiribiti what it is now." Barasa laments.

"Oh, wait a minute...," says Salama to Siti. "Do you remember the story Mzee Alamini was telling us few days ago about a man who was bruised and broken that came into Kiribiti many, many years ago?"

"YES, I REMEMBER. YOU ARE RIGHT. SO, THAT MAN

WAS BARASA'S GREAT-GREAT-GRANDFATHER?" Says Siti.

"I think so. Let's listen more." Says Salama.

The monkey jumps off Salama and snarls at Barasa.

KWAAAAA

"HE EVEN STOLE THIS POOR MONKEY," Salama speaks out.

"AWAY FROM ME!" Barasa flings his hand to hit the

monkey. The monkey runs back to Salama, who quickly picks him up and cuddles him.

Barasa continues, "When the time came for me to enjoy my fathers' hard work, you refused to allow me. I was entitled to half of every crop harvested, but you all said **'NO'** to me.

'Barasa, go and work, Barasa, join the men hunting', was the song all of you were singing to me. He says mockingly.

"EVERYTHING YOU HAVE BELONGS TO ME!"

He shouts in annoyance.

"And one day, I overheard one of you calling me **UGLY**. Me, Barasa, Ugly! You want to see ugly? I will show you what ugly really is!" Barasa's eyes turn red.

He continues. "You all said I was causing a lot of trouble in the village.

YOU ALL BANISHED ME!

NOW IT IS TIME FOR ME TO REVENGE!

GIVE ME MY MONSTER SUIT, WHEN I WEAR IT, I BECOME FEARLESS!"

Barasa snatches off the heavy suit from a guard's hands and wears it in a haste.

"YOU CANNOT TOUCH ME NOW, I AM BARASA THE MONSTER"

He says.

"I AM GOING TO DEAL WITH YOU ONE BY ONE.

MOOHOOHAHA"

All the villagers cower. Some hug themselves, others run away and shut the door behind them. Okello panics, he gnashes his teeth.

Salama shouts out,

"IT'S NOTHING! IT IS ONLY A MERE COSTUME. IT HAS HUMPS SO THAT IT CAN COVER HIS HUNCH BACK, A BEAK TO COVER HIS LONG NOSE AND THE FUR TO DISGUISE IN THE BUSH. DON'T LET HIM GO."

As Barasa bawls at the villagers, a hefty guard comes close to him and gives him a great big kick. He flies so high into the sky…

… that his monster suit rips off him and he lands right inside the cell.

"EXACTLY WHERE HE NEEDS TO BE!" smiles Okello.

"HURRAY!!!

WE ARE FREE FROM TROUBLE NOW,"

the villagers cheer.

"Kiribiti will now be as peaceful as it used to be." Says Mama Fifi as she bends to be at the same height as Salama. "Well done Salama, you did a great job, but next time be more careful. I am not happy you went back into the forest after you have been warned not to. However, I am happy it's for a good cause and it all turned out well."

"Ok Mama Fifi, I am sorry I had to go back into the forest, but I knew I could do it. You have always taught me to be brave! Remember those days Mama Fifi, when you showed me some good fight moves? I haven't forgotten grandma; I still have those moves."

Salama's face lights up, she jumps up and kicks the air.

EEAYA!,"

"Hahaha Salama, **FIGHT MOVES**. You are a wonderful child, Salama. I love you, my girl." Says Mama Fifi with glee.

"AHEM," Okello clears his throat and says "All these

celebrations would not have been possible without one brave little girl here in Kiribiti. Kiribiti appreciates you Salama and we would like to reward you for your bravery. Salama risked her life to save other children, and not only the children, but all of us. On behalf of our land, I present you this mysterious crystal we were given as a gift many years ago.

IT IS NOW YOURS FOREVER!"

"HONGERA SHUJAA! HURRAY!!!"

The villagers cheer on.

Glossary

Cathedral – a large place of worship for Christians

Fire torch – a stick that can be lit on one end

Havoc – trouble or something causing damage

Hut – a small shelter made with straws and mud

Mancala – a two player wooden game with stones

Paradise - A place of pleasure

Rickety - Shaky; not firm

Tranquil - Peaceful

Swahili

Amina - Amen

Hapana - No

Hongera Shujaa! – Congratulations hero!

Kuna mtu hapa – There is somebody here

Kwanini – Why

Moto - Fire

Msaada - Help

Msitu - Forest

Nenda -- Go

Ni Mimi – It is me

Njo Nje – Come on out

Onyesha uso wako – Show your face

Sawasawa – Exactly

Tumbili - Monkey

Unaweza kunisikia? – Can you hear me?

Ugali – African meal made from maize flour, eaten with fish or beef stew

Bwana bibi – Boss lady

Printed in Poland
by Amazon Fulfillment
Poland Sp. z o.o., Wrocław

61762974R00070